# LULU
## AND THE
## BRONTOSAURUS

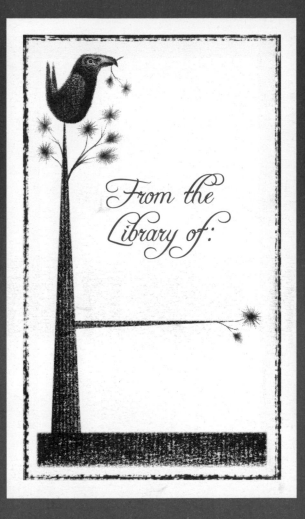

*From the*
*Library of:*

# LULU

## AND THE
## BRONTOSAURUS

JUDITH VIORST

*illustrated by* LANE SMITH

**SIMON AND SCHUSTER**

First published in Great Britain in 2010 by Simon and Schuster UK Ltd
A CBS COMPANY

Simon & Schuster UK Ltd
1st Floor, 222 Gray's Inn Road, London WC1X 8HB

Originally published in 2010 by Atheneum Books for Young Readers, an
imprint of Simon & Schuster Children's Publishing Division, 1230 Avenue
of Americas, New York, BY 10020

www.simonandschuster.co.uk

Text copyright © Judith Viorst 2010
Illustrations copyright © Lane Smith 2010
Book design by Molly Leach

A CIP catalogue record for this book is available from the British Library.

ISBN 978-0-85707-147-7

1 3 5 7 9 10 8 6 4 2

Printed in the UK by CPI William Clowes, Beccles NR34 7TL

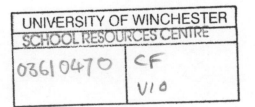

For Nathaniel Redding Gwadz Viorst
and Benjamin Carlo Gwadz Viorst,
who helped me write this story
—J. V.


For Molly
—L. S.

# OKAY! *All right! You don't*

*I know* that people and dinosaurs have never lived on Earth at the same time. And *I know* that dinosaurs aren't living now. I even also know that paleontologists (folks who study dinosaurs) decided that a dinosaur that was once called a brontosaurus (a very nice name) shouldn't be called brontosaurus anymore, and *have to tell me!* I know!

changed it to apatosaurus
(a kind of ugly name). But since
I'm the person writing this story,
I get to choose what I write, and
I'm writing about a girl and a
B R O N T O S A U R U S.
So if you don't want to read this
book, you can close it up right
now – you won't hurt my
feelings. And if you still want
to read it, here goes:

chapter one

*There* once was a girl named Lulu, and she was a pain. She wasn't a pain in the elbow. She wasn't a pain in the knee. She was a pain – a very big pain – in the

b u t t .

Now, Lulu was an only child, and her mum and her dad gave her everything she wanted. And guess what? Lulu wanted EVERYTHING. Tons of sweets. Tons of toys. Tons of watching tons of cartoons on TV. And if her mum and her dad ever said (and they hardly ever said it), "Sorry, darling, we think you've had enough," Lulu would screech until the lightbulbs burst and throw herself down on the floor, and then she would kick her heels and wave her arms. And pretty soon her mum and her dad would say, "Well, just this once," and let her have whatever it was she wanted.

chapter two

*Two* weeks before Lulu's birthday, she announced to her mum and her dad that she wanted a brontosaurus for her b-day present. What did she say? What? A brontosaurus? Yes, she wanted a brontosaurus for a pet. At first Lulu's mum and her dad just thought she was making a little joke. And then they saw – oh, horrors! – that she was serious.

They patiently explained that a brontosaurus is a quite enormous dinosaur who lives in forests, not in people's houses.

(Is that where a brontosaurus would live? In a forest? I'm afraid that I'm not absolutely sure. But since I'm the person writing this story, I'm putting this brontosaurus in a forest, along with a lot of other wild beasts that I'm absolutely sure did not live on Earth when dinosaurs were there.)

Anyway, Lulu's mum and her dad continued explaining to her, although a brontosaurus is into eating plants, not animals (including human animals like Lulu), and although it is cute (in a long-necked, pinheaded way), it is much too huge and too wild to be a good pet.

A dog,
a cat,
a goldfish,
a bird,
a gerbil,
a guinea pig, yes.

A brontosaurus?

Definitely no.

chapter three

*No,* Her mum and her dad were telling Lulu no? Lulu wasn't used to hearing no. And she hated – she really hated – hearing no. To show how much she hated it, she screeched and screeched and screeched until all the lightbulbs in the living room burst.

"I WANT A BRONTOSAURUS FOR MY BIRTHDAY PRESENT," she said in between screeches.

"I WANT A BRONTOSAURUS FOR A PET."

"Well, maybe we could get you a nice pet rabbit," said her mum.

"Or even," said her dad, "a nice pet rat."

"Nonononononono!" screeched Lulu.

# "I WANT A BRONTOSAURUS FOR A PET."

Then she threw herself down on the floor and kicked her heels and waved her arms and screeched some more.

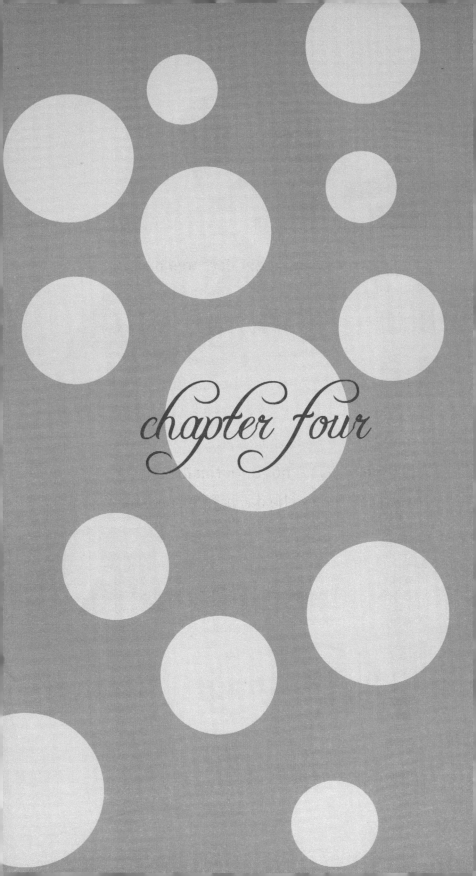

chapter four

*Four* days, eight days, ten days, twelve days passed. Lulu kept saying, "I WANT A BRONTOSAURUS." Her mum and her dad just kept on saying no. Lulu kept screeching and throwing herself on the floor and kicking her heels and waving her arms. Lulu's mum and her dad kept saying no. Until finally, on the thirteenth day, the day before Lulu's birthday, right after lunch, Lulu said to her mum and her dad, "Okay then, foo on you." (She had terrible manners.) "If you aren't going to get me a brontosaurus, I'm going out and getting one for myself."

Lulu packed a small suitcase, said
goodbye to her mum and her dad, and
walked out the door.

And they let her go! Partly because they thought she'd change her mind and come running back home in about two minutes. And partly because it was nice to not have her screeching and kicking and waving and being a pain.

"Let's have a cup of tea and a couple of biscuits," Lulu's mum said to her dad.

"Excellent idea," her dad replied.

So they went into the kitchen and started munching on some biscuits and sipping tea. And pretty soon they'd forgotten all about Lulu.

chapter five

*But* Lulu hadn't forgotten that she was going to get herself a brontosaurus. And luckily for Lulu, there was a great big forest not too far from her house. The animals in that forest had never bothered anybody, because nobody had ever bothered them. But – watch out, creatures! – here came Lulu, trudging through the forest, swinging her small suitcase back and forth, and – in a quite loud voice that was sure to wake the napping animals from their naps – singing this song:

*I'm gonna, I'm gonna, I'm gonna,*

*gonna get*

*A bronto-bronto-bronto*
*Brontosaurus for a pet.*

*I'm gonna, I'm gonna,*
*I'm gonna, gonna get*

*A bronto-bronto-bronto*
*Brontosaurus for a pet.*

The forest that Lulu was trudging through was overgrown with trees whose branches scratched her face and whose roots she tripped over. But Lulu hardly noticed, because she was thinking just one thought, and you know what that was.

So on she went, swinging her suitcase
and singing her song too loudly and
annoying all the creatures in the forest,
and being the same big pain out there
that she was back home in her house,

until. . .

Slithering down from the branch of a
tree came a long, fat, brown-black snake,
who had been peacefully snoozing until
Lulu woke him up. Sleepy and grumpy
and hissing an exceedingly nasty hiss,
he wrapped himself around Lulu, around
and around and tighter and tighter, and
told her she'd really be sorry that she had
woken him.

"I'm going to squeeze you dead," he said.

(Okay, so snakes don't talk. But in my story they do.)

And Lulu said, "Not if I squeeze you deader."

So Lulu squeezed the snake – hard! – and the snake yelled, "Ow!" and quickly unwrapped himself from Lulu. And Lulu, wiping some snake sweat from the palms of her snake-squeezing hands, went on trudging deeper into the forest.

chapter six

I'm gonna, I'm gonna,
I'm gonna, gonna get
A bronto-bronto-bronto
Brontosaurus for a pet.
I'm gonna, I'm gonna,
I'm gonna, gonna get
A bronto-bronto-bronto
Brontosaurus for a pet.

Singing her brontosaurus song in a louder and louder voice, Lulu was waking up nappers all over the forest. Some were annoyed. Some were extremely annoyed.

Among the extremely annoyed was a silky, slinky lady tiger, who yawned and stretched and rubbed her bright green eyes, and then, with a ferocious roar, sprang out from behind some trees and pounced on Lulu.

"You're a big pain," the tiger said, "so I'm going to eat you up for my afternoon snack."

"Uh-uh," said Lulu. "I'm bonking you on the head." And swinging, swinging with all her might, Lulu bonked the tiger with her suitcase.

The tiger yelled, "Ow!" and fell down in a pitiful black-and-orange-striped heap on the forest floor. Lulu brushed off a few tiger hairs that were stuck to the side of her tiger-bonking suitcase and went on trudging deeper into the forest.

chapter seven

As the afternoon turned into late afternoon and then into early evening, Lulu trudged ever deeper into the forest. When she felt hungry, she opened her suitcase and took out a sandwich.

When she felt cold, she took out a
sweater and socks. And when it got
buggy, she opened her suitcase and
took out some bug spray and sprayed.
She was feeling a little tired, but she
kept trudging and swinging her suitcase
and singing her song.

I'm gonna, I'm gonna,
  I'm gonna, gonna get
A bronto-bronto-bronto
  Brontosaurus for a pet.
I'm gonna, I'm gonna,
  I'm gonna, gonna get
A bronto-bronto-bronto
  Brontosaurus for a pet.

Now, a big black bear who liked listening to the music that insects make in the early evening couldn't hear their song because Lulu's was louder. Plus, a lot of the insects were deader because Lulu kept on spraying them with her spray. This made him mad. Then madder. Then madder than that. He growled a thunderous growl and then he lumbered heavily down the forest path and stood on his two hind legs in front of Lulu. Waving a big claw-y paw in her face, he said, "You're interrupting my favourite programme." (Please don't give me an argument. In my story, bears are allowed to have favorite programmes.) "So I'm going to scratch you to pieces with my claws."

Lulu glared at the big black bear and put her hands on her hips. "Nobody's scratching *me*," she told the bear. Then she jumped – as high as she possibly could – in the air. Then she landed – as hard as she possibly could – on his foot.

The bear yelled, "Ow!" and went limping away, as fast as a bear could limp with one stomped foot. And, after shaking some broken, bear toenails off the bottoms of her bear-stomping shoes, Lulu went trudging deeper into the forest.

chapter eight

*Lulu* was now in the deepest, darkest, quietest part of the forest. It was getting quite late and she was getting quite tired. She took her sleeping bag out of her suitcase, spread it on the ground and lay down to sleep. But before she slept, she sang her song once more.

*I'm gonna, I'm gonna,*

*I'm gonna, gonna get*

*A bronto-bronto-bronto*

*Brontosaurus for a pet.*

*I'm gonna, I'm gonna,*

*I'm gonna, gonna get*

*A bronto-bronto-bronto*

*Brontosaurus for a pet.*

Actually, she never even got to sing
the last line because, before she could
get to it, she was asleep.

# chapter eight and one half

dawn Lulu woke to the sound of birds calling to one another, and the dusky-musky smell of the forest floor, and the feel of a gentle late-summer breeze blowing across her face, and the taste (because she hadn't bothered to brush her teeth before bedtime) of yesterday's sandwich. She also woke to the sight of something so huge, so enormous, so utterly gigantic that she thought – no, she was sure – that she was still dreaming. It looked like a mountain, except this mountain had legs, a very long neck, and a very small head. It was (as I'm sure you've already figured out) the brontosaurus that Lulu had been searching for.

chapter nine

*Lulu* closed, then opened, then closed, then opened her eyes again and decided she wasn't dreaming after all. She quickly climbed out of her sleeping bag and announced to the brontosaurus, "It's my birthday today and – just in time! – I've found you."

"No, *I've* found *you*," the brontosaurus told Lulu. "And I'd like to wish you a very happy birthday."

"Oh, it will be very happy," Lulu said
to the brontosaurus, "because you," –
she patted his ankle, because his ankle
was as high as she could reach –"you
are the pet I'm getting for my birthday."

The brontosaurus bent down his
neck so his face was close to Lulu's.
He looked at her back to front and head
to toes, sniffing at her carefully with
his brontosaurus nose and making a
rumbling noise (nobody knows how
dinosaurs sound, but in my story they
rumble) and slowly nodding, nodding
his pinheaded head.

"A pet," he said to Lulu, after he'd nodded for a while, "is a very good thing."

"A very, very good thing," Lulu replied. She opened up her suitcase and went digging around inside and pulled out a white leather collar, which she fastened around the brontosaurus's neck.

"Now I'll just attach this lead," – she dug some more and found a long, long lead in her suitcase –"and take you home with me."

Lulu attached the lead to the collar, feeling so pleased with herself that she sang a whole new brontosaurus song.

I got it! I got it! I got
What I wanted to get,
A bronto-bronto-bronto
Brontosaurus for a pet.
I got it! I got it! I got
What I wanted to get,
A bronto-bronto-bronto
Brontosaurus for a pet.

She would have kept feeling pleased
with herself, except now the brontosaurus
was shaking his head. And now, in his
rumbling voice, he was saying, "No." He
was saying no and shaking his head until
the collar and lead flew off. "No," he said,
"I don't wish to be your pet."

Lulu, remember, hated hearing no. She
really, really hated hearing no. So she
screeched until all the birds fled from the
trees, and then she threw herself down on
the forest floor, and then she kicked her
heels and waved her arms.

The brontosaurus waited patiently, without saying one more word, until she had stopped with the screeching and kicking and waving. "Finished now?" he quite politely asked.

"Maybe I am," Lulu said. "And maybe I'm not. It all depends," – and here she shook a finger right in the brontosaurus's face; this girl was a pain, but she wasn't a scaredy-cat – "it all depends on whether you stop saying no and start saying yes to being my pet."

The brontosaurus shook his head some more. Lulu thought about screeching and so forth some more. But instead she said, in a very snippy voice, "Now listen here, you were the one who said to me just a minute ago that – and I quote – 'A PET IS A VERY GOOD THING.'"

"That's what I said," the brontosaurus admitted.

"So what," Lulu asked, "is your problem, Mr B?"

"No problem," he answered. "Just a misunderstanding. Because when I said that a pet is a very good thing, I didn't mean I wanted to be *your* pet. I meant that *you'd* be a very good pet for *me*."

chapter ten

*Lulu's* eyes were two round Os of amazement. She tried to speak, but at first no words came out. Then finally she was able to say, in a squeaky, amazed kind of voice, "I don't think I heard what I think I just heard, Mr B."

"You did indeed," the brontosaurus replied.

"Well, if I did," – Lulu's voice was back to being its old bossy self again—"well, if I did, I've got some news for you. A person HAS a pet. An animal IS a pet. A person can't be an animal's pet, E V E R."

"And I have some news for you," the brontosaurus said to Lulu, except that he spoke more politely than Lulu had done. "You're about to be the first person – ever – to be an animal's pet. Congratulations and, once again, happy birthday."

He reached out a hand (or whatever you want to call it) and gently scooped Lulu off the forest floor.

62

He then plunked her gently down where his back met his neck. "Hold on tight, little pet," he said to Lulu. "I'll pull off some leaves from the tops of the trees for your breakfast. And then I'm taking you home to live with me."

"No!" yelled Lulu. "No! No! No! A billion zillion times no."

"Yes, yes, yes," the brontosaurus replied. "I'll feed you and pat you and play with you and treat you very nicely. And all I'll expect from you is to sit and roll over and fetch a ball and do cute tricks." (What did he think she was, some kind of dog-girl? I really don't know; I can't read a dinosaur's mind.)

Lulu thought about screeching and throwing herself on the forest floor, except that the forest floor was a long way down. She thought about squeezing the dinosaur dead, except that she needed both hands to hang on to his neck. She thought about swinging and swinging her suitcase and bonking him on the head, except that she'd left her suitcase under a tree. And she couldn't stomp on his foot, because his feet were far too far from his back, where he'd plunked her.

Then Lulu started to think that the only thing further from where the brontosaurus had plunked her was her home, her home where her mum and her dad were waiting, her very own home where no one – not even when she was being a pain (which was most of the time) – had ever, ever expected her to sit and roll over and fetch and do cute tricks.

"I want to go home to *my* house," Lulu told the brontosaurus, then added in a lot-less-bossier voice, "Please let me go back to my house, Mr B."

This was maybe the very first time in Lulu's entire life that she, without being told, had used the P word. And yet the brontosaurus shook his head no. "Once you get used to it," he kindly told Lulu, "I truly believe that you'll like being a pet."

Lulu imagined being a pet in the house of this brontosaurus and never seeing her mum or her dad again. She imagined eating leaves and doing cute tricks. And she said to herself that if only she could turn today into yesterday, she wouldn't go looking for dinosaurs in the forest and she wouldn't say, "Foo on you" to her mum and her dad.

She was feeling especially sorry that she had ever said, "Foo on you" to her mum and her dad.

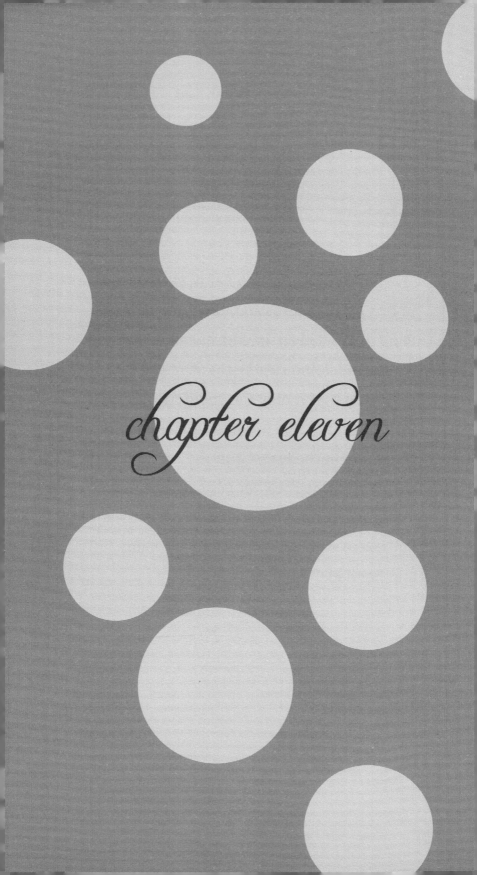

chapter eleven

*The* brontosaurus pulled leaves off the trees and was offering them to Lulu. She grabbed them and threw them angrily away.

"A simple 'no, thank you' will do," the brontosaurus said to Lulu. "And I really liked that 'please' you used before."

"So please please please, let me please go home!" yelled Lulu.

"Your yelling is hurting my ears," said the dinosaur. "But I have to admit that even if you had asked me softly and sweetly, I still would want to keep you here with me. I've been lonely, and a pet is a very good thing."

For hours and hours and hours, from early morning till just past noon, Lulu kept telling the brontosaurus he had to let her go home, and the brontosaurus kept telling Lulu no. He also kept assuring her that he'd do his absolute best to make her happy. He spoke in such a kind and nice and polite and patient voice that after a while Lulu was talking, not yelling. And after a while she was talking softly and sweetly. And pretty soon after that, she started to cry.

Yes, Lulu started to cry. And it wasn't very often that Lulu cried. She'd rather screech till the lightbulbs burst and all of that other stuff, but right now she didn't feel screechy – she felt teary. And so she cried and cried and cried, soaking the brontosaurus with her tears.

He patiently waited as Lulu continued soaking him, and the forest floor, with her tears. He patiently waited some more and then he said, "I'm sorry I'm making you cry, little pet, but I won't be changing my mind. Would you like a tissue?"

Lulu now understood that no matter how hard she cried and how nice this dinosaur was, he was determined to keep her as his pet. And she now understood that if she was determined to NOT be his pet, she would have to escape. She cried just a little bit longer, but while she was crying on the outside, she was – on the inside – making a getaway plan.

Sniffing a watery sniff, Lulu said to the brontosaurus, "Thank you, Mr B, I do need some tissues. If you'll just let me down on the forest floor for a minute, I'm sure I can find a box of them in my suitcase."

The brontosaurus lowered his head and his neck to the floor of the forest. Lulu slid off, stood up and smiled a small smile. She walked to her suitcase, opened it, poked around for a while and found (are you surprised?) a big box of tissues.

But instead of taking the tissues out,
she put her sleeping bag in, snapped her
suitcase shut and. . . started running.

The brontosaurus stood stiff and still,
as if he'd been glued to the ground. And
then he started running after Lulu. But
Lulu had darted off the path, into the
heart of the forest, into a part of the
forest where the trees grew so close
together that a creature as huge as this
dinosaur could not fit. She zigged and
she zagged and she zigged and she
zagged through those close-together
trees while the brontosaurus looked for
spaces to squeeze through.

He was trying his hardest to catch her –
as hard as a mountain-size creature can
try – but she was leaving him further and
further behind. "Come back, little pet,
come back," Lulu could hear him calling,
first loudly, then softer and softer. "Come
back, little pet. I know you'll be happy
with me."

"Come back, little pet. . ." His voice
grew ever softer. And soon she could not
hear his voice anymore.

Since Lulu could not hear his voice
anymore, she stopped running and
started walking. She tromped through
the forest in silence, heading for home.

But she wasn't swinging her suitcase
and she wasn't singing her song, and
although she very much wanted to see
her mum and her dad again, and very
much wanted NOT to be a pet, she felt
kind of bad about the brontosaurus.
(And so do I. Because even though I'm
the person writing this story, I don't
like leaving him all alone, sadly calling,
"Come back, little pet. Come back.")

chapter twelve

*But* then, after maybe an hour, Lulu suddenly heard a different voice, a not-so-friendly voice, saying, "Hold it right there." And standing up on his two hind legs, and blocking her path through the forest, stood the black bear she had stomped on yesterday.

"*You* hold it right there," said Lulu, "and please," – there was that P word again—"don't keep shaking your claw-y paws at me. If I have to stomp you, I'll stomp you, but I'd really rather not stomp you. I'd rather," – she opened her suitcase and took out a jar of golden honey – "give you this if you'll please get out of my way." (What's going on with Lulu? She'd rather not *stomp* him?)

The bear took the jar of honey, opened the top, dipped in his paw and slurpily licked it, mumbling something that sort of sounded like "Thank you." Dipping and licking and slurping, he hurried out of Lulu's path. And she continued tromping through the forest.

Until. . . another familiar, another not-too-friendly voice said, "This time I'm eating you before you bonk me." And there was the tiger, the silky, slinky tiger of yesterday, ready to pounce on her.

"Forget the eating and bonking," said Lulu, "and try on this beautiful scarf." She pulled a long, floaty, bright green scarf from her suitcase. "It matches your eyes, and I'll give it to you if you'll please get out of my way." And the tiger, happily wrapping the eye-matching scarf around her black-and-orange-striped neck, growled something that sounded like "Thank you," and slunk away. And Lulu continued tromping through the forest.

Until. . . well, what do you think she met next? A wolf? A giraffe? A lion? Don't be ridiculous. She met – of course she met; what else? – the snake, who was hissing an even nastier hiss than he'd hissed the day before and warning her, "This time *I'll* be the tighter squeezer."

Lulu, looking disgusted, told him, "Nobody's squeezing anybody. All I'm doing is getting home today." Then she reached in her suitcase and pulled out a small flowered rug and explained to the snake, "This is for you if you'll please get out of my way. A soft rug to rest on whenever you feel like resting."

The snake took the rug in his mouth
and tried (at least I think he tried) to say
thank you to Lulu, though it's hard to tell
when a mouth is full of rug. In any case,
he went slithering off wherever a snake
goes slithering. And Lulu continued
tromping through the forest.

# chapter thirteen

*It* wasn't too much later that Lulu could see that she was nearly out of the forest. She was happy that soon she would be with her mum and her dad. But along with feeling happy, she was also feeling sad when she thought of the brontosaurus she'd left behind. As a matter of fact, she pictured the poor lonely dinosaur so clearly in her mind that it almost seemed he was standing there, just outside of the forest, waiting for her.

A N D   H E   W A S !

Was Lulu shocked? You bet! "What –
what – what," she asked, "are you doing
here, Mr B?"

"I found a shortcut," the brontosaurus
replied.

Lulu smiled a soft, sweet smile, then
shook her head and sighed. And then she
said (and even though I'm the person
writing this story, I truly don't know why
she's saying it in rhyme):

*"Please try to understand, Mr B,*
*That I cannot be your pet.*
*Even though you're the nicest*
*Brontosaurus I ever met.*
*And if you take me away with you,*
*I'll keep on running back home —*
*Every chance that I get."*

(Not a bad rhyme, though
that last line's a little lumpy.)

"I already figured that out while I was waiting for you," the brontosaurus told Lulu. "I do understand that you can't be my pet. But please understand that I can't be *your* pet either."

Well, Lulu understood and the brontosaurus understood. It seemed there was only one thing left to do. So they stood there, quietly looking at each other for a moment. And then they did it.

The brontosaurus bent his long neck till his face was close to Lulu's. He kissed her gently on the cheek and said, "Happy birthday, little pet. . . and goodbye."

Lulu put her arms around the brontosaurus's neck. She kissed him gently on his nose and said, "Don't be too lonely, Mr B. . . and goodbye."

Then she slowly walked down the road that would take her home.

Then he slowly walked down the road that would take him home.

And although Lulu and the brontosaurus remembered each other forever, they never ever saw each other again.

The
(maybe)
End

# chapter thirteen
## (again)

*Wait!* I'm really not all that sure about this ending. It may be a little too mushy, a little too sad. But since I'm the person writing this story, I'm writing another ending and you can decide which one you'd rather have:

Well, Lulu understood and the brontosaurus understood that neither of them could be the other's pet. But why should that mean that they had to say goodbye? "Come with me and I'll give you a piece of my birthday cake," said Lulu.

"I'd like that," the dinosaur said. "May I give you a ride?"

And Lulu arrived at her house, riding happily on the back of the brontosaurus.

When her mum and her dad heard the noise of a dinosaur clomping into their garden, they remembered Lulu and they remembered her birthday. Lucky for all, her cake had already been made. "Don't worry. He isn't my pet," Lulu said. "He's only going to stay here for a piece of cake and a glass of lemonade. But he's kind of a lonely guy, and I would like to invite him back for Christmas dinner."

From that time on, the brontosaurus came to Lulu's house for her birthday, Christmas, and any special occasion. And sometimes she visited his house, though (since she didn't like eating leaves) she always brought a suitcase of sandwiches. On one very special birthday she not only invited her friend the brontosaurus, but also the snake and the tiger and the bear.
And the brontosaurus noticed that whenever Lulu asked anyone for anything, she always said please.

The
End
(maybe)

# chapter thirteen
## (yet again)

*Hmmm.* I'm still not totally satisfied. I'm going to try once more, because I think I need to answer certain questions. Like: Were Lulu's mum and her dad worried sick when she didn't come home that night? Had they bought her a present for her birthday? Did she completely stop being a pain and turn into polite? And how did all that stuff fit into her suitcase? I'm going to answer these questions and when I'm done you will have your choice of *three* different endings.

Well, Lulu understood and the brontosaurus understood that, though they couldn't be pets, they could be friends. So Lulu invited the brontosaurus back to her house for some birthday cake and introduced him to her mum and her dad. They hadn't been waiting and worrying and wondering where she was because they had fallen asleep sipping their tea, and they didn't open their eyes until the brontosaurus, with Lulu riding on his back, came clomp-clomp-clomping into their front garden.

They gave her a silver necklace for her birthday.

She sang them a whole new brontosaurus song:

I didn't, I didn't,
I didn't, didn't get
A bronto-bronto-bronto
Brontosaurus for a pet.
I didn't, I didn't,
I didn't, didn't get
A bronto-bronto-bronto
Brontosaurus for a pet.

"It sure looks like you've brought one home," Lulu's mum said to Lulu.

"And we still say no, you can't have one," said her dad. And both of them waited for Lulu to screech and throw herself down on the floor and kick her heels and wave her arms in the air.

Except she didn't.

"What happened to the screeching?" asked her quite astonished mum.

And her dad asked, "What about throwing yourself on the floor?"

Lulu replied, very dignified, "I'm one year older today, and I'm not doing that kid stuff anymore."

"And she says a very nice 'please,'" said the brontosaurus.

After the cake and the lemonade, the dinosaur said goodbye, but he would return for many holiday visits. Sometimes the snake and tiger and bear came too. Although she kept getting older, Lulu never turned into perfect. She still – though less and less often – sometimes screeched and forgot about "please" though she never again in her life said, "Foo on you." But she mainly wasn't a pain and the brontosaurus was mainly not lonely anymore.

As for how all that stuff fitted into Lulu's suitcase, I'm sorry to say that I don't have a clue. I am, after all, just the person who's writing this story.

*The*

*End*